the
Witch
with no broom

Written and illustrated by
Carlos Rubio

Balboa Press books may be ordered through booksellers or by contacting:

Balboa Press
A Division of Hay House
1663 Liberty Drive
Bloomington, IN 47403
www.balboapress.com
844-682-1282

ISBN: 978-1-9822-4403-3 (sc)
ISBN: 978-1-9822-4404-0 (e)

Library of Congress Control Number: 2020904066

Print information available on the last page.

Balboa Press rev. date: 09/08/2021

BALBOA.PRESS
A DIVISION OF HAY HOUSE

To Nina Sofia

It's Halloween time
and witches are out,
hundreds of them
flying about.

We've been told they are scary, spooky and mean,
but some are the nicest that you've ever seen.

Since I was a baby
they've appeared in my room,
so here's the story of
the witch with no broom.

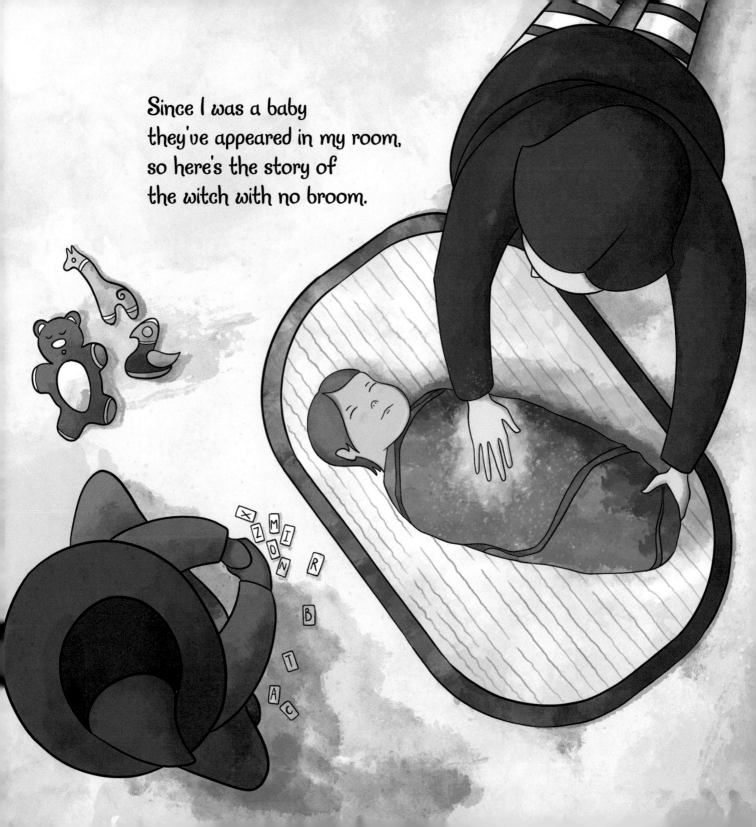

I was playing outside
one full moon night,
when a shooting star
blew up by my kite.

From the glowing sphere
something came near,
and I trembled in fear
as the form was unclear.

My worry disappeared
when the figure I saw
was no monster or creature,
but a kind, sweet lady
like mommy or my teacher.

And when she spoke
instead of a spell,
she uttered the words,
"Hello, I'm Snowell."

Her hat was small,
and not of dark leather,
but a cute silky cap with
a flower and feather.

A silvery white dress
was cut at her knee,
and from a golden sash
hung a pouch and a key.

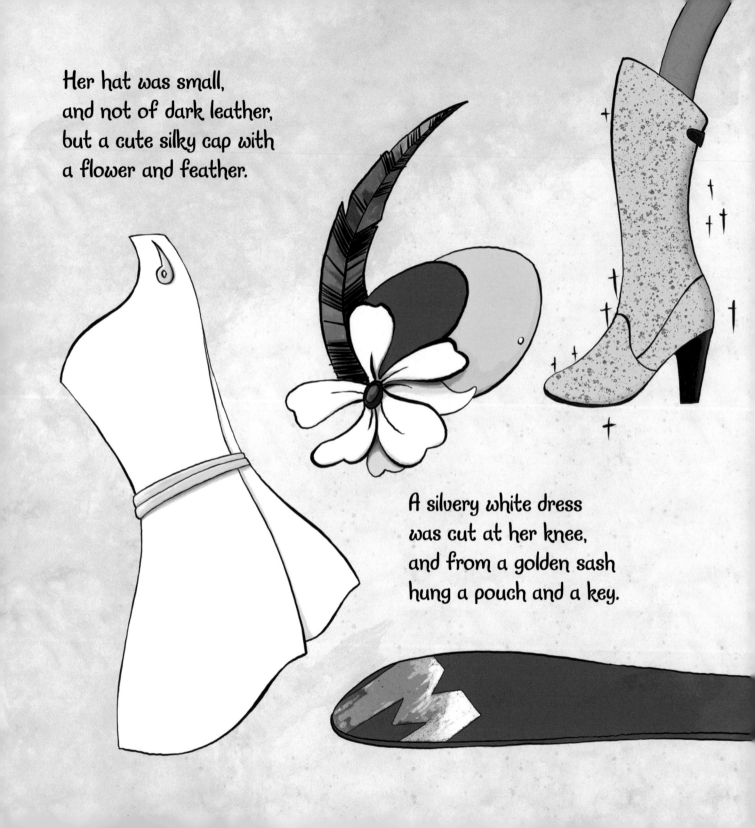

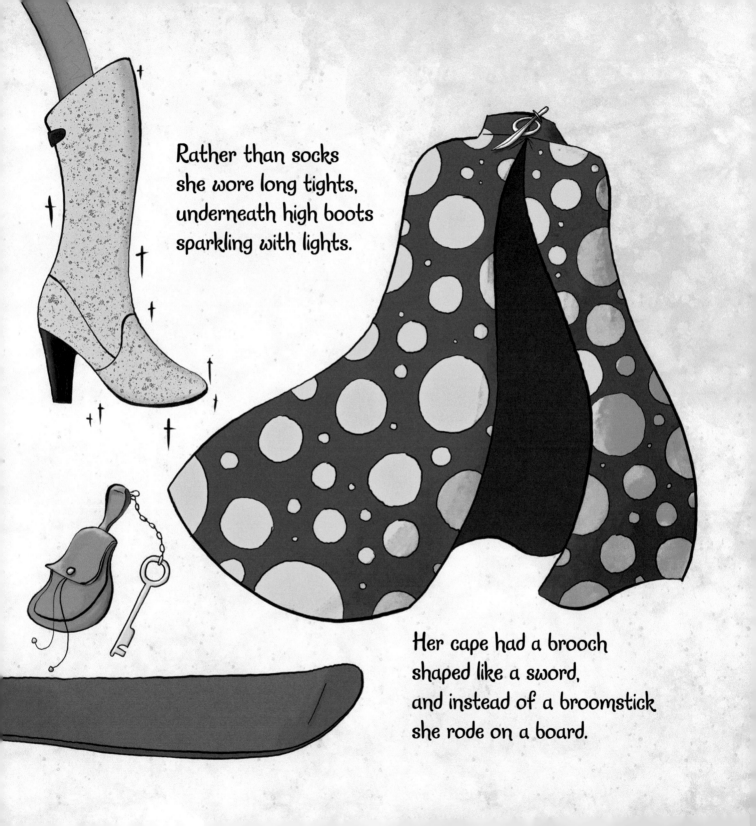

Rather than socks
she wore long tights,
underneath high boots
sparkling with lights.

Her cape had a brooch
shaped like a sword,
and instead of a broomstick
she rode on a board.

Snowell was no stranger,
I knew it when she smiled.
She visited my crib
when I was a little child.

She invited me to her world as I was almost eight.
I agreed and we flew up going fast and straight.

With a gesture of her hand
a portal she created.
By wishing a wish,
her power was activated.

Once in the tunnel
with a flip and a twist,
we surfed onto her planet
covered in mist.

"Welcome to Magicca!"
she pointed to the ground,
as a beautiful forest
showed up all around.

"Today we won't land, we'll just fly instead.
As you get older we'll stay longer," she said.

With a yell and a tuck
we quickly dove down,
coming closer to treetops
and roofs of a town.

The woods were yellow, orange and red,
with houses made of candy and fences of bread.

On meadows and in valleys
animals grazed and flew,
even some winged unicorns
flapped into view.

There were three-legged runners
and long-necked dinos,
spiky-tailed dragons and
double-horned rhinos.

Pink was the water
black were the dunes,
purple was the grass
and brown were the moons.

The tiny pale sun produced a midday twilight,
the reason witches love dusk, dawn and night.

All this was amazing!
There was so much to see,
but Snowell said it was time
to return with me.

We joined other witches up high in the sky,
and together we crafted an opening nearby.

Dressed as funny clowns and in formal gowns,
these people rode on planes, rockets, carpets and trains.

To my city we came back
with a loud crack of thunder,
dancing, jumping and twirling
all excited with wonder.

Snowell's quick arrival could be seen from the streets,
but instead of shock and panic children greeted us with treats.

A cheerful crowd surrounded us
as we landed in the park,
surprised at my excitement
to ride with a witch in the dark.

Printed in the United States
by Baker & Taylor Publisher Services